HOLLY KELLER

Geraldine's Blanket

Greenwillow Books New York

 A Children's Choice® Book Club Edition from Educational Products Inc.

FOR MY MOTHER

Geraldine had a pink blanket.

Aunt Bessie sent it when Geraldine
was a little baby.

And Mama put it in her crib.

Even when she got bigger,
Geraldine loved her blanket.

She took it with her everywhere.

"You won't need your blanket at the market," Mama said.
"I will," Geraldine insisted.

And she always found a use for it.

When the blanket got dirty,
Geraldine helped wash it.

When there were holes,
Mama covered them with patches.

And when the edges were all frayed,
Mama trimmed them.

But Geraldine only loved it more.

"There's hardly any blanket left," Papa said.
He was getting cross.

Geraldine covered her ears.

"It looks silly," Mama said.

"Then don't look at me," Geraldine said, stamping her foot.

Mama tried to hide the blanket in the closet.

But Geraldine found it right away.

She kept it pinned to her dress all day.

And tucked it under her pillow at night.

Mama and Papa talked in whispers.

And at Christmas there was a new present
from Aunt Bessie.

The doll's name was Rosa,
and Geraldine loved her.
"But I still want my blanket," she said.

"No," Papa said.
"No," Mama agreed.

Geraldine knew what to do.

"There," she said when she had finished.
"Now Rosa has the blanket and I have Rosa."

Mama didn't know what to say.
Papa scratched his head.

And Geraldine took Rosa out to play.